best wishes
Rajani
Jan 15, 2020

Rajani Kanth

A Day in the Life

Limited Special Edition. No. 13 of 20 Paperbacks

Rajani Kanth

A Day in the Life

AUSTIN MACAULEY PUBLISHERS™

LONDON · CAMBRIDGE · NEW YORK · SHARJAH

A CIP catalogue record for this title is available from the British Library.

ISBN 9781787109896 (Paperback)
ISBN 9781787109902 (E-Book)

www.austinmacauley.com

First Published (2019)
Austin Macauley Publishers Ltd
25 Canada Square
Canary Wharf
London
E14 5LQ

For Shikha – Antara, Indrina, Malini, Anjana and Cory

It is perhaps unavoidable that most story-telling is autobiography.

A Day in the Life, leastways in metaphor, is just that, conceived at the borders of the real and the surreal.

I need to thank the lengthy tribe of my oppressors since childhood, whose tribe never seems to diminish, who kindled the waking spirit that informs the story, spread over as it is with shades of tristesse, if at varying levels of depth and intensity.

I must also thank the invisible, yet ever-present, muse that moved this work, written headlong in one short weekend in Utah, from the dusky cloister of distal invention to pen and paper.

More mundanely, I am grateful to Austin Macauley for seeing some literary merit in it; to its editors from Kirsten Jolly to Rebecca Ponting, who offered support along the way; and to Vinh Tran and Norma Clarke, the production coordinators, who patiently put up with my (artistic) excesses.

I can only beg pardon of others at the press that I am omitting to mention, solely out of ignorance, who, if more anonymously, helped oversee this book through to the light of day.

We live in terrible times, fraught with risk, uncertainty, and schism; if art can heal, even partly, and very personally, some of the grave breaches of spirit in our time, both extant and still to come, then *A Day in the Life* would have served a useful social purpose.

If not, it is no more than yet another gust in the wind, eddy in the vast current that, inexorably, and willy-nilly, propels us all to the unchartable limbo of posterity.

Absit Omen.

Table of Contents

CHAPTER ONE

It wasn't his fault.

The morning was cold and bleak, and the traffic noisier than usual.

Looking out the window, the grey overhang of vapors almost hit you in the face with its biting stench.

Pulling the drapes down seemed far the better idea, though the room got even darker.

Sighing, he looked over.

The coffee machine she had left on had by now turned itself off.

Some machine, he thought, trying to think forwards for me too.

Things were foul enough: why not try a sip?

The coffee was cold and bitter, and he almost spat it out.

Smart machines! What a joke!

The cat purred by the bedside.

He looked at it.

What do you want, Shakespeare?

Here, try some coffee today. Might like it.

The cat drank it up, but doubtfully, and then looked up at him.

He shrugged.

Now don't you start, he said, you're a good kitty: don't go putting on no airs.

Whew.

Another day.

Should he, or shouldn't he?

In another minute, her alarm would go off.

Hang it, he hated alarms.

They jolted you.

Someone across the hall had an alarm that played Verdi.

Hers just blasted you off like something out of Cape Canaveral.

He waited.

The piercing blast made the cat streak underneath the bed.

He jumped up at the alarm and smothered it in a tight embrace.

It still sounded.

He buried his head in the pillow until it stopped.

Now it definitely was another day.

Unless something really unusual happened.

And he could make it happen.

Couldn't he?

You bet.

Good morning, sang a voice at the door as a hand tapped lightly on it.

I wish she wouldn't, he thought.

Not today. Please.

Pretty Please?

Not that he didn't like little old ladies.

Just ones that trilled down the stairs on the one day he wasn't up to it.

Out on the street the drilling began, rattling the walls.

God.

CHAPTER TWO

He looked out at the bay, as the cars cruised past him.

The buses swung great big loops to bypass standing cars.

The wind chilled his bones.

The bay was fogged up.

There was nothing one could see.

The foghorn blasted his ears.

I must be calm, he said to himself.

No, he had been calm for 30 long years.

Not today. Uh-huh.

Well, maybe.

Calm down. It's just another day.

No, it was not.

How could it be?

A smile creased his face.

His face muscles stiffened, unaccustomed to such tension.

His smile broadened.

And he laughed out loud.

So loud, passersby avoided him fearfully.

He smiled at them benignly.

They were okay.

So was he, really.

Guess things could be lighter.

Take it easy, they had always said to him.

Now he knew. Yeah.

He was going to take it easy.

Real easy. Ha-ha!

He bent down and petted a dog on a leash that snarled at him.

Its owner scowled, too.

He smiled at them both.

Take it easy, he said to them, as they hurried past.

Look at you, he whispered to himself.

You are taking it easy.

In this beautiful world.

On a beautiful morning.

Okay, so it was a mite foggy and cold. So what!!

How easy it all was! And it had never occurred to him!

He looked around. Do these people know?

I mean, do they?

It was so easy. He wished they knew.

Should he tell them?

No. There's a time for everything.

They'd find out one day.

Just like he had.

Yeah.

They could wait.

He walked on, almost jauntily.

He was making his day.

Nothing could stop him now.

CHAPTER THREE

The other night.

His brow darkened, and he frowned.

A little girl, walking by, smiled at him.

He stood transfixed.

She had smiled at him: and he had had on the darkest scowl.

Heck.

He turned around to smile back, but she was far away.

Hang it. It was the other night he was scowling about.

And now that little girl would walk away thinking he was just an awful, ugly man.

He ran back part of the way, but she was nowhere in sight.

He had lost her.

Just like Shiela, that night.

He leaned on a lamppost, sighing.

Passersby avoided him. Soon, a cop would walk up to him,

swinging a baton, or worse.

It didn't matter.

He lit a cigarette.

He had never smoked before.

He still had her cigarette case.

What's the point of waiting for you, she had said, turning the coffee machine on.

She, not he, was the coffee drinker.

You're going no place, never. You can't even get it on. A girl's gotta have something, don't you think?

But I like you.

And what does that do for me? What does that do? Nothing. Nothing. You couldn't even take me out to dinner!

I don't go out to dinner.

You see…

Why can't we just be…?

Be…?

Yeah.

Be what?

Oh…you don't get it sometimes.

You never spoke a truer word. I don't get it. Know what I

22

mean…? You get it? I get nothing…

Me…am I nothing?

I need more… heck, you need more than that…we both do…I waited long enough.

For what?

For something to happen. For something new. Something different. I'm tired. I'm tired of the same old crap. It's getting like something stupid…I want better.

Oh, no.

Goodbye. It's best for both of us.

What?

I gotta go. Now. Cold turkey. Or, it'll never be.

You mean…

Yeah…

No…

And guess who I'm gonna be seein', starting tomorrow? Just guess!

Who?

Lenny. That's who!

Lenny!

You betcha…least he's a real guy, warts n' all…g'bye…I need to live in the real world…

But...

Bang. The door slammed in his face. The coffee machine turned itself off, discreetly.

CHAPTER FOUR

The real world. What was that?

I need a drink, he said to himself.

Yeah, I know. It's only nine in the morning. And he didn't drink. So what?

Who makes the rules, anyway?

He stepped into a bar.

I need a drink, he said.

What'll it be?

The usual.

The barman eyed him, shrugged, and poured him one.

Bars suck, he thought. 'Specially in the mornings.

The winos in there stank like pigs.

He sat apart and had a drink. Yecch. He could a puked.

The TV was on. A talk show.

Johnny Candid telling us all how to live.

The secret, said the creep, mousse dripping from his hairline, was in self-worth. Gotta have that.

Self-worth! Think he means net worth.

The barman grinned.

Think he's got a point, though, said the barman.

No, he said.

The barman erased the grin.

Want another? he asked.

'Course not…have I ever gone seconds on you?

The barman grimaced, and counted the change.

He walked out the bar.

Self-worth. How the heck was he to have it?

Where could he buy it?

The street seemed way too bright as he walked out.

CHAPTER FIVE

He wished he hadn't stopped off for that drink. He wondered what it was.

Sure tasted godawful.

His head throbbed a little. Self-worth! What did they know?

His mother. She used to go on about that.

You gotta have self-respect, or you ain't nobody.

Well, she was right. He was nobody.

Then the teachers. The trouble with you is…

What did they know?

He knew. He always did. Nobody else could be you!

But, boy! Did they never stop trying!!

I mean, what right did they have? Where did they get off?

Well, he could tell them…just let 'em ask.

A man walked right into him.

Watch where you're goin', bud, said the assailant, tersely.

Some nerve.

Why didn't *he* watch where he was goin'!!

The gall.

Okay, so he was a mite unsteady.

Make allowances, darn it!!

That's the problem, ain't it!!

Yeah!!

Trouble is nobody makes allowances no more.

Look at Shiela.

Oh, heck. He shouldn't have remembered Shiela.

You're with someone years and years, and just when you're all cozy and comfortable they wanna split up and start over again.

Make allowances, he turned and said to the man.

But the man had walked on.

You would make allowances…if you knew the consequences.

Ha-ha! He laughed.

If they only knew!!

Boy, were they gonna find out!!

CHAPTER SIX

This walk was proving taxing.

He was not used to it, having taken a bus for years.

He hated buses, of course, but cars were unaffordable; just the parking rates could kill you.

No, he was quite lazy.

Why take on more stress and call it stress-relief? His heart was just fine. He ate prudently.

Heck, he virtually lived by the book, one might say.

But now they were writing new books.

So everyone from four to a hundred was running around in spandex feeling superior to those that didn't.

Silly. Really stupid.

Feeling good couldn't result from feeling rotten; running five miles was enough to make your heart wanna fall out your mouth.

He remembered the day he dropped his wallet in a grocery store and had to run back for it.

The sweating and the panting.

Just awful.

Of course, you couldn't convince Shiela not to be a goose. She was hooked on the media.

If they told her to do stomach exercises, she did it.

Religiously, tears streaming down her face.

She bought every pill they sold her.

Trusting. You know. A dupe.

Whew!

Why couldn't people figure for themselves?

Look at him: he was savvy.

Okay, so nobody else thought so.

But no one could put one over him.

Let them try. Nope.

But this walking bit, that wasn't smart.

But it was deliberate.

Today had to be different.

Shiela. She should see him now. They all should.

Maybe even his mother, rest her soul.

It would sure wow them.
You bet.

CHAPTER SEVEN

Hey mister, can I engage you for just one moment?

He stopped.

This wasn't your ordinary street talk: 'engage' you!

Well, whaddoyouknow?

Who was this guy?

He peered at him. He had on a clean suit and a black collar.

Oh, Christ. A minister!

He shouldn't have stopped. Ministers always talked funny.

I am obliged to you, sir, for making time for me. I assure you it will not be time wasted. I have come to speak to you of the coming of the Lord.

Of who?

Whom…the good Lord, sir. Our Maker: Jesus Christ in heaven. He is to walk amongst us again, as was promised in the Bible.

Okay by me.

You don't understand, sir. The Son of God is to be with us

again this Xmas. It is written.

By whom?

By the founder of our faith, the Right Honorable Josiah Temple Goodman.

Never heard of him.

The prophet lives in Cleveland, Ohio, sir. Now if you would support his ministry…

Say what?

If you would make a very small donation…

But he had walked on. To be goosed in broad daylight in the name of the Lord!

Boy, did you have to be careful!

Hucksters, everywhere.

He turned his head, and murmured.

Con artist!

But the Servant of the Prophet had just buttonholed another.

He was already history.

CHAPTER EIGHT

People didn't make time anymore. Wasn't that the damnedest?

I mean, they just didn't.

Take Lenny, at work. Nice guy.

Shared lunch with him for years.

But just the other day, when he tried to explain to him why he was feeling lousy lately, just got up and said: sorry you're having trouble, guy, but I gotta go. Work, you know. Talk to you later. Bye.

Talk to you later!

When? Next Xmas, maybe.

Work! Work could wait, couldn't it?

I mean what's life all about, he would like to know?

Busy. Yeah, everyone's busy.

Even little old ladies in spandex, running down sidewalks.

So, no one has time for nobody.

Except the shrinks. They got loads of time.

Pay those turkeys some and you could chew their ears out until the stopwatch beeped, when they rose abruptly, opened the door, shook hands, and bounced you out.

Who was listening to you?

Shiela would listen, of course. But was she really listening?

Couldn't have been, or else…

What a world!

And who made it that way?

I mean this is all new, ain't it?

His mama had time, for everyone. Even the milkman got cookies and milk!

Only house he knew where tradespeople visited, not simply made deliveries.

But she was from another planet.

A planet that, like her, was no more. Enough to break your heart.

Darn it, it got him upset.

You'se all messed up, he muttered. You hear me? Messed up!

Pedestrians now steered clear of him, like he was some drunken bum, or sump'n.

Boy, was he upset!

He could just…

Oh, well. In time. In time.

CHAPTER NINE

His boss.

That was another story.

I ain't hiring you 'cause you're any good, mind. I'm hirin' you 'cause you're cheap. In fact, the cheapest. How you make do beats me. But I ain't complainin'. Just keep out of my hair, 'specially if you screw up. Okay?

Amazing!

What a thing to say to a new employee! You're no good…but you're cheap, sucker.

Of course, he was cheap.

Heck, he could live on half of what he got paid.

Maybe even a quarter.

Heck, anyone could, if they only stopped to figure things out.

You got no ambition, said Lenny, when he had gotten passed over for a promotion that went to Ricky, the other office boy.

You ain't even mad that he got the job.

'Course he had no ambition. Anybody could see that!

No mystery to it, darn it!

How much ambition could you snake up delivering packages? All he wanted was…well, to be sort of left alone, minding his own business.

And, boy, did that rattle people!

You ain't getting this promotion, said his boss.

Okay, boss.

Okay, boss…?

Yeah. Fine. Okay. No big deal.

No big deal?

Nope.

You ain't sore?

Sore? Heck, no. Why should I be?

Jesus Christ.

What?

Nothin'. You can go now.

Okay. Bye.

His boss was shaking his head.

Sore? Why?

Couldn't they figure he was happy, just being able to come to work every day and say hello, and make coffee in the coffee machine in the hall?

'Course, he didn't drink any coffee.

Why do you make coffee, then, if you don't drink it?

He made it for Lenny, for the boss, whoever. He just liked making coffee.

Heck, he couldn't care less if he never got a dime more than he was getting now.

Couldn't they figure all that?

What could be more obvious?

CHAPTER TEN

There was baloney everywhere.

I mean, think about it. Everywhere!

Just look up at the hoardings.

We do it all for you!

Yeah, right!

Or: can I help you?

Darn it, they couldn't even help themselves, unless it was to someone else's portion!

He looked up at the hoardings.

The smiling faces. How come people always smiled in cigarette ads?

He never met a smoker who did. Baleful, spiteful creatures all.

That treacherous flash of teeth!

He felt he was ready to sound off at the first person today who flashed him a phony smile.

Get real!

What's there to smile about in their world, he'd like to know!

I mean, the birds, and the bees, and the flowers were all dead, weren't they?

What was there left to smile at?

Asphalt? Studios on the seven hundredth floor? Automatic condom machines?

I mean, come on.

It was Grim.

A child kicking a ball came running up, ready to cross the road. Horns tooted.

People yelled from car windows.

The child, unnerved, picked up the ball and ran home.

He watched.

Yeah, there were a few things they couldn't yet kill off. But they were trying, weren't they?

And, one day, it would all…

Poor kid. Safer at home bouncing the ball off the stove than out in this jungle.

Poor kid!

Yeah, he shoulda stayed home, too. No point to even what he had in mind.

But, his mind was made up.

For once, he had to do what he had to do.

CHAPTER ELEVEN

There was a movie he saw once. Three men were beating up on a fourth.

He didn't know why.

It was one of those *cinema verite* types. In French.

But it went on and on until he had to get up and walk out.

Nauseating.

Yet the director was, obviously, getting off on it. And the usual cinema buffs watched, like zombies.

He coulda thrown up on the screen.

God, it was awful.

Well, life was something like that.

You saw it all around you. Just like that movie.

And it went on and on and on.

Difference is, you couldn't walk out. No Exit.

Or, was there?

Well, he was determined to find out.

Nope, he lied.

He knew there was.

Always.

An Exit, with your own personal name on it.

Sure.

Heck, he should almost be happy or sump'n, just for knowin' it.

Perhaps he was.

CHAPTER TWELVE

A woman smiled at him.

It got him edgy.

I mean, she looked like someone's wife or somethin'.

And that smile wasn't just a smile you flash the world to say you're happy.

It said: come to me. I like you. What say…?

He couldn't stomach that.

I mean, it's about faith.

You're with someone. Have some faith.

Once he or she walks out, then go flirt your socks off, but not while…

He stared back at her, smilelessly, shaking his head. She winked at him.

What a world!

Ain't there enough trouble to wanna go looking for it?

I mean: what is it with some of these people?

She didn't look like she was rich and bored.

In fact, he never knew anyone rich who looked bored.

In fact, they all looked like they'd had so much fun they were about ready to die from it.

Rich and bored!

What a fantasy. Yeah, just what penniless writers could cook up for a potboiler.

Yvette was rich. She was bored. She stroked her Persian while smoking a Murad, looking listlessly out the window in Monte Carlo…

Yeah, right!

He'd be bored straight to death in that still. Stroking her Persian, my eye!

Oh, well…

He was ready to make allowances.

So a rich, bored woman smiled at him today.

Dear diary…so what!

Shiela was the only woman he knew.

And she was gone.

What a life!

As he shook his head, the woman now brushed past him, smiling suggestively.

What the heck!!

She turned and looked at him again, then walked on with the gait of a swan.

Whew!!

He shoulda known! A hooker! A hooker!

And here he thought…

Just business. That's all it was. What a business!!

His head swam.

He was not used to articulating so many ordinary thoughts.

It was proving quite a day.

Almost like even Providence was on to him.

CHAPTER THIRTEEN

A two-mile walk, and it was taking an eternity.

Darned city streets. Traffic. The jostling.

The red lights. In his world, all traffic lights would be green.

Whose world was it anyway?

Of course he could don spandex and run down the street, but…

A leisurely morning walk was what he wished; and that's what he would have, come preachers, hookers, and what have you.

The business at hand demanded it.

Business. A bad word.

It suggested smiles drying up, muscles tensing, detached coolness.

No, he was incapable of it.

He was soft. Emotional, that's what he was.

No head for business, his mother would say, sighing, as if she had one.

But, yeah, she was right.

Dealing fast and loose was not his style.
He could toss the chips; he didn't much care where they fell.

And the chips were about to fall.

Hey, mister.

What? A little girl! Again!

Hi. Say, mister would you buy my flowers?

Uh…

He saw the child's mother standing by the wall looking on.
Some sort of a charity collection, no doubt.

Why, sure, honey…how much?

A dollar apiece, sir.

A dollar apiece! Great Godfrey!

Still, he couldn't disappoint the kid.

The child smiled up, sweetly.

How many would you like, sir?

Uh…how about one…uh, two…yeah, I'll take two.

Just two, sir?

Yeah, two's fine…okay, make it three.

Okay, sir. Here you go.

The child held out the flowers.

He handed over the three dollars and the child gave him a heartbreaker of a smile.

What a sweet kid!

He watched her walk back to her mother, wreathed in smiles.
The mother smiled, too.

God, what a kid!!

He looked around at the ugly street.

No place for a sunny little flower like that, was it?

Whew!

The world had to be made safe…for kids like her.

He turned back and smiled, waving.

A little pudgy arm waved back.

God!

Take good care of her, mom, he yelled to her mother, who looked at him rather oddly.

She's an angel.

The mother waved goodbye, but hastily.

Bet she thinks I am a kook too, he thought.

What a world!

CHAPTER FOURTEEN

Only a few more blocks, and the Day would get Done.

He thought of his kitten.

Mus'n't forget the cat chow.

He hoped his cat wouldn't be sick from that coffee. He knew he would have. That cat chow was a must.

But would there be time?

This was a strange day. Altogether strange.

Yes, he had faced off a barman. Cool as an ice cube.

And almost pushed a hostile pedestrian out of his way.

Could it all be him?

A cigarette, then a drink?

Wait, there was more. Yes, lots more.

Good god! How could he be so blind?

He nearly sat down on the sidewalk, overcome by emotion.

The sun broke, shining on him alone.

He looked up.

Bad day to play games, god, he thought. Very bad day.

Yes, now he understood.

So, even today, the day he had planned out for himself had been anticipated.

Almost thwarted?

No way. Not even god could do that.

How could he have been so blind?

A preacher, a hooker, and a little angel!

God might as well have hit him on the head with a golden cross.

Sending Messengers.

Decoys? Sirens?

He had read the Eastern tale of Siddhartha, the young Buddha.

And now this replay, on a busy city street!

Too late, dear god!

You had a lifetime to send me messages, but all you did was slip me a series of Mickey Finns.

And now that I am taking charge. Now that I am taking charge. Now that I am taking charge.

Heck, no. It was too late. Nice try, Jehovah!

He had to laugh. This was funny.

CHAPTER FIFTEEN

His mother.

Yeah, she was something else.

He coulda been all kinds of things. But she held him back.

Sort of a moral restraint.

Which was just as well.

Bless her soul.

Was she watching from the high heavens?

Let her.

God couldn't have scared him. But she could.

It was a moral thing.

She was maybe better than god, for being like Him despite being only a little old lady.

He didn't have a choice. She did.

And, what a woman!

Now, if She were to come walking up to him, he might have considered listening, even if she weren't his mother.

See, god: you ain't half as smart as you'd like us all to think!

A woman detached herself from the crowd and came straight up to him.

He broke out in a sweat.

She had on a scarf like his mother wore. And that coat!

She was coming right on up to him.

Could it be…?

God…he heaved a sigh of relief.

She brushed past him to get to the mailbox he had been standing by.

No, it wasn't HER. Just an old woman. In a hurry.

But it was close. Too close.

Goshdarnit! This was turning into a passion play.

A few more blocks.

How much longer could it take?

Perhaps he should turn around and go home.

But his feet kept moving on.

Oh, well.

CHAPTER SIXTEEN

So it was Lenny Shiela wanted to see.

Swell. Let her.

He wasn't sore. Why should he be?

Lenny was okay. A sharp cookie, one might say.

But so what?

It was okay.

Someday, he'd be probably make boss.

Yeah.

And Shiela would be just thrilled!

Say, this wasn't all bad. Shiela would get…finally…what she wanted.

Maybe he'd take her out to dinner.

Nah. He was too darned cheap.

Frozen TV dinners, probably. And home videos.

They'd be sitting on the couch in Lenny's living room while…

No…this was getting difficult.

No. It couldn't be?

Was he just a tad jealous?

No way! Right?

Wrong.

Heck.

Rats.

No.

It was all wrong.

Shiela wasn't Lenny's type at all.

Darn it!

Yep. It was going to be a very hard day.

Until it was over.

CHAPTER SEVENTEEN

He had never felt like this.

Why?

What was so special about it?

So, Shiela left him.

Big deal.

Stand up for something, said his mother.

He had laughed.

Why? He had asked.

What's the point?

And his mother had just looked at him in her tearful way.

So Shiela left him.

Coulda happened anytime. To anyone.

Why sweat?

On account of Lenny, said his Bad Self.

So what?

Not Lenny, goshdarnit!

He leaned on a wall covered with hoardings.

So, she left him for Lenny.

Lenny!

Lenny was…well, just your ordinary, everyday, amoral thief…

But attractive, in a dark way.

He had to admit it.

Okay, so he wasn't that slick…

Besides, he didn't have that special Plus.

That extra that made dames go for it.

He knew that.

He may be stupid, but he wasn't dumb.

Even the secretaries – a hard bitten lot, usually – went for him.

He had boasted of taking one home every night…

And now he was taking Shiela…

No!

But why?

'Cause he was a loser.

And now, a sore loser.

Man, was today a special day, or what?

Everything was comin' out feelin' different.

You'se changed, pal, he said to himself. Don't you see?

Of course, he could see.

Anybody could be *not* Junior. Just look around you.

And now, he was gonna be just like 'em all.

But, he didn't have to like it.

No one could make him like it.

No one.

He could see to that, anytime.

Yeah.

No one's gonna be pushin' him around no more.

You betcha.

CHAPTER EIGHTEEN

He needed another cigarette.

But you don't smoke!

So he felt like it, today: what's the problem?

He bought a pack from a machine and lit one, casually.

Felt good.

Took a puff.

Didn't feel so good.

In fact, it tasted like charcoal.

If that's what Marlboro country was like, he wouldn't be applying for no goshdarned citizenship!

Jesus, what some folks could get away with.

Like Lenny. With Shiela.

His Shiela.

What a sweetie she was, really.

He wasn't all that deserving of her himself.

But that con artist Lennie…no way!

Yeah, a man-to-man talk.

Maybe even a showdown.

He lit another cigarette, and puffed real hard.

That wasn't so bad.

Now if he could only get on a horse, and be someplace in Wyoming, or Montana, it would all fit.

Watch out, Lenny.

He could play hardball, too.

You better believe it.

CHAPTER NINETEEN

Go on, said his mother. Tell Tommy not to take your ball away again.

No, I won't.

Why not?

'Cause I don't care if he does. It's only a ball, for Chrissakes.

Don't swear.

Sorry, mom. But they all do.

Junior! She always called him that, since childhood.

Hmm?

Oh, never mind.

Okay. Say, mom?

Yeah?

Could you, maybe, buy me another ball…?

Oh, shoot.

But she bought him another anyway, and still another,

when Tommy took it away again.

That was his mother.

An angel.

She never made him feel small. Even when he made major mistakes.

Now, where did his boss get off?

You're no damn good, he had said.

Was that sweet?

Nope, positively hurtful.

No excuse for rudeness. That's what his mother used to say.

Mr. Boss?

Yeah.

That wasn't very nice.

What?

Telling me I'm an idiot.

What!

Y'know, the other day. In front of everyone.

Hey.

What?

Get out!

Okay.

Now!

Okay. But it still wasn't very nice…

Out!

That's how the interview might have gone, had he requested it.

But he hadn't requested it.

CHAPTER TWENTY

The day his mother died, he had been out walking in the park, at dawn.

Came home, and the neighbors had gathered.

She died peacefully, in her sleep.

She had said goodnight to him fondly, he remembered.

Maybe he shoulda listened to her.

All the things she said.

Maybe things might have turned out differently.

But as it is, she died feeling sad on his account.

That wasn't right.

Jeez!

Maybe he'd been a chump all his life!

And now…but it was all too late!

He could be the Marlboro man himself, but she'd never know.

He let the tears fall, as he tossed the pack in the trash-bin.

He had never really cried over Mother before.

Sorry, Mom.

If only…

But…

Life's a bitch, and then your mother dies…

He wished he could just walk back home, jump in bed, and go to sleep.

But there was no turning back.

The die was cast.

CHAPTER TWENTY-ONE

He met Shiela in the park, that same day.

Shiela had spandex on, and was running.

As it happened, she ran straight into him.

He was knocked over into the small duck pond.

He couldn't swim, though the pond was not very deep.

Shiela had to fish him out.

Even gave him mouth-to-mouth.

I am so terribly sorry!

O, it's nothin'.

Nothin'. You nearly drowned! Shall I take you to a doctor? Do you need anything?

A doctor. Christ, no. I'm fine. Just a bit wet.

Look. Come over to my car. I got a blanket in the trunk. Maybe I can give you a ride home.

Okay.

So she had. And then stayed on a while, when he had found

out about his mom.

Fate, she had said, later.

She had saved his life. He always owed her that.

Heck, he hoped she'd be happy now. At last.

Okay: so let it be Lenny!

CHAPTER TWENTY-TWO

Not that his boss was much better.

That office party, before Xmas.

Shiela had come, against his will, to the party.

That was Shiela. She loved parties.

His boss had come over to them, already over the top with his drinks.

And who's the lovely lady?

It's my...friend.

Well, aren't you gonna introduce me?

This here, Shiela, is my boss.

And a great guy, too, said his boss. Pleased to meet you, Shiela.

Say, the boss turned to him.

What?

Can you get me a drink?

You have one.

Oh...no, no...not this; get me a pink lady.

A pink lady?

Yeah, a pink lady. Just ask the bartender.

Okay.

So he left to get him a pink lady.

When he got back, they were gone. He looked all over.

It was no use.

Then Lenny came over, grinning.

What's the matter? You look sorta confused.

It's Shiela...she was just here...

Oh, ho...laughed Lenny. She's over there.

Where?

Lenny pointed to the boss's office, grinning.

Gee, thanks, Lenny.

He walked over to the door and knocked.

Whozzit?

It's me.

Go away.

I'm looking for Shiela.

He could hear laughter.

He heard his boss say. He's looking for Shiela…ha-ha!

Shiela was heard chuckling, too.

He had pushed the door ajar. The two were sitting atop the table, cozy as anything.

Now, said his boss, crossly. It says 'private' up on the door. Can't you read?

Come on, Shiela. Let's go, he had said.

Shiela made a face, but came on.

Did you want your pink lady?

I think I just had me one…ha-ha!

He set down the drink tray.

Bye, boss.

They walked out.

He's okay, said Shiela, quite tipsy.

Oh yeah? he said.

CHAPTER TWENTY-THREE

His father was like his boss.

Always laughing.

He laughed a lot at him.

Don't laugh at Junior, said his mother.

But he's so funny, he would say, and laugh again.

What're you gonna do, Junior? asked his dad.

Do?

Yeah, I mean when you're all grown up?

Don't know.

Well, it's about time you started making plans.

Why?

Why? 'Cause that's just the way it is. Everybody makes plans.

Did you?

Why, sure.

What did you plan?

Well...uh...this and that...look: we're talking about you, not me. Take a tip from me. You wanna be a conductor on a train? Big job. Big responsibility. Big bucks.

No. I hate trains.

Why?

They go too fast, and they can jump off the tracks.

How about a fireman?

No. Don't much like fires.

A cop?

Hate guns.

Shoot, what do you wanna be?

A volunteer traffic-warden.

What?

They help little kids cross the street.

Yeah?

I like their uniforms.

You like their uniforms?

And I like little kids.

Oh, brother. My only son - and he wants to be Mickey Mouse. Jeez.

Leave him alone, said his mother.

Junior, said his dad, you're weird. Know that? Weird. Better shape up, n' soon. It's a bad world out there. Gotta be smart, or you're dead.

What does he mean? he asked his mother.

Don't pay him no notice, said his mother, he's just joshin' ya.

That same night his father got killed in a train accident.

He was a train conductor.

It's just you and me, now, Junior, said his mother, hugging him, and crying.

Don't you cry, mama, he had told her. I'll take care of you.

And that's what he told anyone who asked him what he wanted to do.

I'm gonna take care of mama, he would say, when I'm all grown up.

CHAPTER TWENTY-FOUR

He was as good as his word.

He made sure his mama had what she wanted.

You can't be fussing over me the whole time, his mother would say.

But I like to, he would say.

Bless you, Junior, she would say, and cry.

She always made him his favorite dish. Potato soup.

Find yourself a nice girl, Junior, and I'll teach her how to make it for you.

I don't want girls, mama, he would say. Girls is trouble.

Who told you that?

Dad used to say that.

Now listen to me, Junior…and his mother would tell him how she wouldn't be here forever.

How he'd need to have a family of his own.

You and me is enough family for me, he would say.

Oh, Junior, she would say, and hug him. And cry.

Why do you cry, mama? Aren't you happy?

I am very happy, she would say.

Yeah, he was happy.

'Cause he made mama happy.

No one could take that away from him.

But they did.

CHAPTER TWENTY-FIVE

You were just a mama's boy, said Shiela.

What's a mama's boy?

You know…

I don't.

Okay…it's boys who can't get over their mamas. Ever.

Why should they?

Oh, Junior.

She called him Junior, too. So did everyone.

Why is that bad?

Junior.

What?

You're just…

What?

Oh, never mind…

No, go on…say it!

Be a man, Junior.

What?

You heard me.

It was just what his dad used to say.

But I am a man.

Yeah, but…

But what…?

Oh, never mind…

CHAPTER TWENTY-SIX

What's a man, Lenny?

What?

What's a man? Shiela keeps wanting me to be a man.

Oh, Yeah?

Yeah. I'm a man, aren't I?

Why, sure you are. Quite a man.

So why does she keep saying that?

Know what?

What?

Next time she says that to you…

Uh-huh.

Tell her to come to Lenny. Tell her Lenny would be happy to be a man…just for her. Any time she wants.

Why should she come to you?

Just kiddin'.

Oh.

Don't worry about it. Someday, she'll figure it out.

Figure what out?

Oh, never mind.

CHAPTER TWENTY-SEVEN

The sun poured through the clouds.

It was getting hot, of a sudden.

The crowds out on the street kept getting bigger.

I gotta make it, he muttered, it's now or never.

It was starting to look like never.

Just a few more blocks, but whew! Was he getting nervous!

But he knew what he had to do.

He wondered what his dad would say, if he could see him now.

I'm real proud of you, my boy!

Nope, nobody had ever said that to him.

Not even mama.

Heck, that was rotten.

Not even his own mama!

You go through life.

Just one life.

And nobody says anything extra nice.

How was he supposed to feel?

I mean, how!

Well, *he* was proud of him.

At least right now.

Didn't need nobody else.

Never did, really.

Except mama.

And Shiela.

Shiela was nice.

Sort of like mama, but cruel.

Yeah, she could be real cruel.

Like Lenny. And the boss. And dad.

He'd bring home a take-out, and she'd toss it in the trash and say:

This is crap, Junior. You expect me to eat crap?

No.

Then why do you bring it home?

I thought you'd like it…

You thought I'd like crap!

No, I meant…

Forget it…I'm going out for a decent meal…one that doesn't come wrapped in styrofoam.

Can I come?

No. I'll see you later.

Ok.

Okay? It's not okay, you moron. Nothing is okay.

And she would slam the door and rush out.

He would feel bad. Very bad.

His mama would never have done that to him.

Shiela was nice.

But she made him unhappy.

CHAPTER TWENTY-EIGHT

And now she was gone.

Maybe forever.

Maybe it was okay.

There was no one left to make him unhappy.

So why was he not happy?

He had always been happy. Sort of.

People said that to him.

You're always cheerful. What's the matter with you?

Of course he was.

The world was beautiful.

He loved the world.

And everything in it.

Well, most everything.

Why shouldn't he be cheerful?

Some people just didn't get it.

And they made others unhappy.

Kids in school did that to him. Said rude things, or stole his lunch.

He could just smile past it all.

In his mind, he sat on top of a hill, looking down on a valley through which a silver river flowed.

It was all very beautiful.

He smiled at what he saw in that valley.

It was a little beyond his school, his neighbors, his family, even himself.

But it always made him happy.

Well, nearly always.

Except today.

Goshdarnit.

Something was wrong.

Seriously wrong.

Whew!

CHAPTER TWENTY-NINE

Shiela had showed him how to make love.

She made love to him one night when she was awful
drunk.

He liked it.

Gotta work harder, kiddo,
she said.

How?

I can't tell you how. You're supposed to know
by now.

I ain't ever made love.

I know.

Maybe I can read a book, or
sump'n.

Maybe.

Was I...bad?

No.

Oh.

Junior…

Huh?

It's okay.

Oh, but you…

Never mind what I said.

Okay. I love you, Shiela.

Yeah. I know.

Shiela went back to her magazine and her cigarette.

CHAPTER THIRTY

Go, Junior, go, they shouted.

It was a school race.

He was a good runner. He nearly always won.

Go, Junior, go.

But he turned and looked at the boy in the next lane.

And that was it.

He suddenly didn't want to win.

Go, Junior, go, the crowd yelled.

He didn't want to go.

He let the boy come abreast, and then let him pass, as his school let out a roar of disappointment.

GO JUNIOR, shouted his coach.

But it was no use.

He was letting the other school win.

Everyone could see that.

Why, Junior? Why did you throw the race?

He shrugged.

Seemed like that other kid needed to win bad.

But it's our school. We lost to them.

Schools are all the same. But that kid, he was different.

Why?

Some people wanna win more than others.

Jeez, Junior. It's a RACE!

Yeah. I know.

Then why did you do it!

Just felt like it.

The boy he let win came up.

Shouldn't have done that, bozo, he said. Now I look like crap.

You're off the team, Junior, said the coach.

Okay.

Get out of my sight.

Okay.

So, nobody understood.

Except mama.

She hugged him.

You're very special, Junior, she said. They don't know
you.

CHAPTER THIRTY-ONE

Yeah, special.

But special what?

Why did people talk down to him?

It didn't matter. He was on his way now, a new man.

Yeah, a new man.

How new?

You'd never guess. Nobody would. But they'd remember. Oh, yes.

Leastways, some would.

Wouldn't they?

He knew they would.

He hoped.

Perhaps.

Maybe?

Heck.

The Circle always kept closing in.

He had to watch his rhythms.

CHAPTER THIRTY-TWO

He turned into an arched doorway.

Then down the stairwell, stopping by a tiny shop.

A scruffy character sat by the counter.

Whaddoyouwant? he said gruffly.

You know, he replied suavely.

Oh, yeah?

Uh-huh.

You the kook who came by Saturday?

Yeah.

Okay, lemme see the dough.

He pulled out a wad.

Better not be fake.

That's all I have.

Swell…hand it over.

He did. The man handed him a parcel, wrapped in

newspaper.

This it?

Yeah.

Okay. Feels like the real thing.

Sure as hell is.

Okay. Bye.

The gruff character resumed his reading.

He walked out into the air again.

Yeah, was this going to be something special!!

Man o man…

If only…

It was okay.

Nobody had to remember. He would know.

That was enough.

CHAPTER THIRTY-THREE

Okay, so Shiela had a right.

She didn't like him, so she split.

But the boss? No, he had no call to fire him.

Just 'cause he went in late Friday.

Junior, you're a damn pain in the butt, he had said.

What did I do?

Nothin'…you never do nothin'…then you come in at 2 in the afternoon.

I got sick in the stomach…

You got sick…hey, I'm sick of you…here's a week's advance. Go home…and don't never come back…get some help.

Help?

Yeah, help, for Chrissakes…

Junior started to cry.

But she left me…

Who left you?

Shiela.

Shiela!

Yeah…so I got like very sad.

Shiela…hmm…got a phone number for her?

Yeah.

Give it to me.

He did.

Okay, now go on, scram.

But…

It's no use…I don't need a gopher no more…go on home.
Buzz off.

And he did, stopping only to tell Lenny.

Too bad, said Lenny.

Yeah.

You'll find somethin' else.

I don't know how to.

The same way you found this one.

I didn't. My mama did the boss's laundry. So she asked
him…

Bye, said Lenny.

Shiela left me.

I know, said Lenny. You're having a bad week.

Yeah.

How is she?

Oh, swell.

Uh-huh.

Is she with you?

Bye, Junior.

Okay. Bye.

CHAPTER THIRTY-FOUR

They brought in a ping-pong coach once, in school.

Nobody could say why.

He had never even seen the game. But it looked like fun.

He wanted to try.

Come on, said the coach, a big Phys. Ed. type of guy flashing eight hundred teeth.

Okay…

Now you hold the bat like this…

But he was playing already. The ball whizzed past the coach, who looked a little dazed.

This is fun.

The coach tried a shot or two, but he was hot and put him clean away. A small crowd gathered.

He was leading 10 to nothing, but didn't know it. The coach did.

Soon, the coach was sweating. And lying about the score, evening it to 10 each, while the crowd booed.

He whizzed past him, despite the creative scorekeeping.

This is fun, he said, gaily.

The coach stopped the game, before it ended.

Oops…sprained my wrist, he said, dropping the bat.

Okay, sorry.

The crowd cheered.

Coach met him in the lockers, later.

You got a lot to learn about the game, he said to him. Don't ever try n' show off. It's bad manners.

I'm sorry, he mumbled.

CHAPTER THIRTY-FIVE

He was paid-up on his rent.

For the month.

A week's wages, in advance.

He was okay.

He coulda gone to the zoo to feed the animals.

He liked animals.

A lot.

Stopped eating hamburgers, when he learnt where they came from.

Or, he coulda gone to the park and sat by the pond, dreamin' of this and that.

But his mind had gotten set.

So here he was, burning shoe leather.

He hoped he was doing the right thing.

He used to be sure of things.

But that was a long time ago.

Not today.

CHAPTER THIRTY-SIX

Where did I go wrong? he thought.

What will they say, when they find out?

Poor kid, they'll shake their heads, didn't have a chance.

It's what they had told him at school.

I don't know…Junior…it's a big world out there…I don't know how you're gonna make out…

His teacher had said that, sadly.

I'll do fine, Ms. Lemming. Don't you worry.

Ms. Lemming had wiped a tear, and hugged him.

She was nice. Almost like his mom.

'Course, he had been right.

He had done well.

Had a job. A girl. Like everyone else.

Everything was just mighty fine, until a few days ago.

Surely, he could do it all over again.

Find a job.

Find another girl.

No, he didn't want another.

No, sir. He was through. Done. Quits.

Shiela had been enough.

Don't know what you'd do without me, Shiela had said.

What?

Never mind. Sort of fate, I suppose, running into you like that…

Running over me…

Yeah.

I fell in love with you…

You fell in the pond, and nearly drowned.

Yeah.

Junior…

Yeah?

Never mind.

No, go on, what?

If I were to leave you…

You're gonna leave me?

No, I mean, if I were to…

Uh-huh.

Could you manage?

Manage?

You know, day-to-day stuff…

Sure…I mean, no…

Shiela looked at him long and hard.

Can't be here forever.

Why not?

Just 'cause.

Okay.

Okay?

Yeah. Okay. Everything'll be okay.

Maybe. But life ain't fair, Junior.

And Shiela had looked at him with that strange expression.

CHAPTER THIRTY-SEVEN

There was some money in his bank account.

Shiela had told him that, the day his mother had died.

He had never gone and looked.

But she had all the bank books.

Somewhere.

One day he would look and see.

It didn't matter right now.

Money never mattered much.

Just needed enough to buy food and sneakers.

His schoolmates had always emptied his pockets out.

He let them. It seemed to make them happy.

He liked to make people happy.

He never needed the money his mother put in his pocket.

Now buy something good to eat, Junior, she'd say.

Don't need any.

Sure you do, all kids do.

Okay.

Shiela never emptied his pockets.

She always paid for everything, even half the rent.

She took some of his money to the bank every week.

Someday you'll need it, she'd say.

Okay.

Now, he didn't remember which bank the money was in.

What a drag!

He'd have to ask Shiela. But how?

Shiela had left him.

For Lenny.

CHAPTER THIRTY-EIGHT

His dad had showed him a gun once.

He couldn't even bear to look at it.

I don't like it, dad.

Why not…she's a beauty!

I hate it.

Why, for Chrissakes!

It…hurts people…don't it?

'Course it does, you dipcake…that's what it's for!

Then I hate it!

Jesus!

Can't imagine anyone spending time making things that hurt people.

His father had stared at him.

Where're you from?

Huh?

I mean, really…

Leave him be, Jack, said his mother.

The kid's plumb crazy…he's always talking stupid.

I says leave him be.

Yeah…I'll leave him be. Everybody'll leave him be. Jesus.

His father left the room in disgust.

It's okay, Junior. Don't feel bad. You'se alright.

But dad…

People think different, son. Is the way it is.

Mom knew everything.

She didn't like guns neither.

CHAPTER THIRTY-NINE

You're strange, said Shiela.

Strange?

Yeah.

Why?

Can't say.

Don't feel strange.

Don't you?

Nope.

But you are.

Whaddayamean?

O forget it…it don't matter.

No, it does. Everybody's sayin' it to me…all the time.

They're right.

Like how?

Okay, we do a test: tell me, Junior…you like to smoke?

Nope.

Like to drink?

Nope.

Like to hang out with the boys?

Nope.

Like girls?

I like you.

That's don't count. Ever think about girls 'fore I came along?

Nope.

See what I mean?

What?

Oh, brother.

Ain't everybody different?

Yeah.

So, I'm not really strange.

You're more than just different.

Dad said I was crazy.

Shoot, you ain't crazy. You're just…

What?

O forget it. This is all stupid.

CHAPTER FORTY

The candy shop was just next door.

Mr. Sikes was always nice to him. Had been so since childhood.

How's it goin', Junior?

Okay, I guess, Mr. Sikes.

Good…what'll it be?

Don't feel like candy today.

What! No way…every day is candy day. Here, try one of these. It's on me.

Really don't feel like it.

Yeah…? So what's the problem, Junior?

Shiela's left me.

Oh yeah?

Uh-huh. And I got fired.

Well, these things happen. Don't take it to heart. There's lots of dames in this world, same as jobs. Look around you.

Uh-huh…but she was a friend.

Yeah…well, there'll be others. World's full of friends, Junior. Just gotta go find 'em.

Don't have no friends.

Nonsense. 'Course you do. I'm your friend.

Could you tell me something, Mr. Sikes?

Yeah, sure.

She told me she was leaving 'cause I was a nobody…

Oh, yeah?

But I am somebody… aren't I?

Yeah, sure you are. She don't know any better. Dames don't know nothin'.

Oh.

Get over it, Junior. These things happen.

CHAPTER FORTY-ONE

Yeah, he could get over it.

Sure, he was somebody.

And did he know it.

Wasn't right the way people…

Yeah, he could get over anything.

He always did.

Except, he didn't want to.

Not this time, anyhow.

See: he had changed, too.

They couldn't push Junior around no more.

Could they?

Least, he hoped they couldn't.

CHAPTER FORTY-TWO

He liked going to the zoo.

He liked animals.

But he didn't like to see them caged.

He talked to them, and they listened back.

What did the monkey say to you? asked Shiela.

Don't be stupid. Monkeys don't talk.

That one did. Come on, I saw it. So what did he say?

He said…O, forget it.

No, come on, Junior. Don't hold back.

Look. What would you say if you was all caged up?

I'd want out.

Sure.

That what he said?

Hmmm.

Wow!

One day I'm gonna...

What?

One day, I'd like to give 'em back their space.

You can't do that!

Why not?

'Cause you ain't god, and they're all caged up.

CHAPTER FORTY-THREE

He felt that way now.

All caged up.

That's what he had been, all his life.

Living behind bars.

Hiding his feelings.

He was sure tired of that.

No more of that.

He was gonna let it all hang out.

He was gonna free himself, too.

It was high time.

CHAPTER FORTY-FOUR

He had reached the entrance to the park.

He walked over to the pond.

Still remembered the spot where Shiela had knocked him down.

He stood and looked at the pond, and the ducks gliding on it.

They sure looked happy.

From a distance, he could hear stirrings from the little zoo nearby.

The animals were hungry, but it wasn't feeding time yet.

They sure didn't sound happy.

Was a shame.

The sun peeped out from under the cloud cover.

God, it was beautiful.

Spring could be real nice at times.

CHAPTER FORTY-FIVE

I see a valley, he said to the ducks who ignored him.

And a silver stream flowing through it.

The valley is all green.

The sky is blue.

And the stream just glides on forever.

I'd like to go on forever.

One of the ducks looked up at him, expectantly.

The valley is my world.

The sky is Shiela.

And the stream is me. You understand?

The duck swam nearer, thinking he had food for it, then turned away.

Guess you don't.

He sighed.

Nobody listens, he said.

The duck turned back round again.

It's okay, he said. I gotta do what I gotta do.

Quack, said the duck.

CHAPTER FORTY-SIX

In summers, he lay out in the park staring up at the sky.

It was always the same.

And he would fall asleep, on and off.

All the light of the day went into his head, filling his dreams.

And the humming of the birds and the bees, and the picnickers all turned into just one soft, low, buzzing sound.

The sound of the universe, he had said to Shiela, who just laughed.

It's true, just like all lights blend into white. All sounds merge.

Oh, yeah?

Yeah…just listen.

But Shiela heard them all separately.

Nope, she said. I can tell 'em all apart.

It's 'cause you don't let 'em in without an ID.

What?

Yeah, you split everythin'.

I do?

Yeah…you break things up.

Oh…and you?

Sort of put 'em back together. It all adds up.

To what?

To just One.

One?

Yeah.

Should have gone to college, she said.

Why?

Just 'cause…

No. College is boring. Like school. People telling you what to do.

CHAPTER FORTY-SEVEN

You don't play with the others, Ms. Lemming would say.

I like to do things by myself.

But in school you come to work and play with other children.

Ms. Lemming.

Yes?

I don't like to come to school.

Oh?

No.

I like to be alone.

Why, Junior?

'Cause then no one tells me what to do, nor calls me names.

Junior, you're a kid. And so long as you're a kid, grown-ups have to tell you what to and what not to do.

Why?

Just the way it is.

I don't like it, Ms. Lemming.

Maybe not. But you gotta do what you gotta do.

CHAPTER FORTY-EIGHT

The clouds and the rain.

He liked to walk home in the rain.

Junior, you're all wet!

I love it, mama.

Why don't you use your umbrella?

I love the rain.

You'll catch your death of cold.

I never get sick, mama. You know that.

Junior…

Mama…things that make me happy can't get me sick.

Junior…

It's true. When it rains and storms, people go in and hide. That's when I love to be out.

Just come in and take those wet duds off.

Okay, mama.

CHAPTER FORTY-NINE

The school had sent him to a psychiatrist once.

Dr. Manx.

Now, sonny, said Dr. Manx, we're going to play a little game. I'll say a word and you say out loud any word that comes into your head.

Okay.

Great: here we go – school.

No.

Home.

Okay.

Lessons.

No.

Friends.

No.

People.

No.

Cat.

Yes.

Dog.

Yes.

Hot dog.

No.

Ice cream.

No.

Soda pop.

No.

Sex?

No.

Doctor.

No.

Junior.

Yes.

Dreams.

Yes.

Colors.

Yes.

The next day his teacher came up to him.

Junior.

Uh-huh?

She just looked at him.

Oh, never mind, she said, sighing.

Okay.

CHAPTER FIFTY

It started to rain.

He sat down and lifted his face up to it.

This is it, he said to himself. Bless me god.

It rained harder.

He shivered.

That Circle again.

It was lifting a little.

Giving him space.

To breathe.

No, he didn't need to do what he was gonna do.

But he'd do it just the same.

For the sake of doing it.

They all said he didn't do nothin' ever.

Well, now he was.

They better make note of that.

Are you watching, Dr. Manx?

CHAPTER FIFTY-ONE

Life's a trap.

You are stuck inside your body.

Unable to get out.

Until you die.

But you struggle, all the time.

Just to get out.

It's the Circle around you.

And you are its Centre.

Sometimes you could make that Circle zip around you like a hula hoop.

Other times it tightened around you like a noose.

Dear god, he said, I wanna get out.

Today.

Now.

This instant.

But it just rained and thundered.

He was going to get very wet.

It was alright with him.

CHAPTER FIFTY-TWO

The real world.

What did they know of the real world?

He knew.

He had always known.

Silently.

Like now, sitting in the rain.

He was the elements.

That was the real world.

That was reality.

Everybody's reality.

Rivers and valleys and trees and rain.

And you.

And living was simply to yield to them.

They took over.

And you went along.

Inside that Circle of yours.

Like protons and neutrons.

Spinning on forever.

CHAPTER FIFTY-THREE

He knew many things.

Life.

And living.

And space.

Most of all, space.

There was nothing else you needed.

Space was the BIG thing.

Even Shiela had trouble understanding it.

There is nothing I want.

Nothing I wish to be.

Just to go on forever.

Nothing is forever, she said.

Everything is…every single thing.

You're gonna be awful surprised…one day, Junior.

No, he was not surprised she left him.

Or that he had gotten fired. Upset, yes; surprised, no.

Well, maybe…just a little.

He was surprised that he was upset.

He was also upset that he was upset.

Rats.

CHAPTER FIFTY-FOUR

Yeah, he moved inside a little Circle.

Like everyone else.

But they thought he was a wacko.

Oh, sure.

He knew that.

He knew that as a little kid.

He didn't need Shiela to tell him that.

But she had to.

Like all of them.

Strange, huh!

What did they know?

He knew, 'cause he listened.

To all the voices that are still when you talk.

And he saw.

Like in a dream.

It was all a dream, wasn't it?

That's all he needed.

That's all anyone needed.

To be free to dream.

And feel the reality.

CHAPTER FIFTY-FIVE

But that's not what they wanted.

They liked to pin it all down, cage everyone up.

Like the big cats that panted, and looked over your head in their squalid cages.

They were looking, and listening, to what was way out there.

Beyond the cages. And the gawking folks who tossed crumbs at them.

To the life they were entitled to.

The life all were entitled to.

But, even in their cages, the animals were free.

Freer than their keepers.

It was the keepers who were chained.

To their chores.

And want of love.

Who were the real animals?

He knew.

It wasn't the kind behind bars.

No, sir.

Their senses were not yet stilled.

CHAPTER FIFTY-SIX

The rain soaked him right through.

A jogger or two watched him from the corners of their eyes as they whizzed past.

They were scared.

He musta looked like a bum.

Like a dope fiend, sitting out there, face up to the falling rain.

If they could only feel what he could.

They wouldn't need to jog.

Or work.

Or do anything.

Just feel the senses splashing inside you, jostling against each other.

Giving you a rush.

Feelings were like an ocean that got bigger as you dived in, and then you just floated.

Carried away.

Yeah.

It was Communion.

The right of all living things.

CHAPTER FIFTY-SEVEN

He had tried to share it with Shiela.

But she was out of synch with her own orbits.

The gravity of her ego pulled her down.

Got her depressed, angry, frustrated.

And she'd drink to feel better.

If only she would give in to that rhythm.

Sort of like a t'ai chi exercise.

Getting you to rotate around your own axis.

Slowly.

We're all in orbits, but if we're out of step we get thrown.

So, she tripped over herself most of the time.

And fell.

Poor Shiela!

She must hurt.

CHAPTER FIFTY-EIGHT

Well, he couldn't point fingers really.

For, today, he too had been thrown.

His mind, for once, wasn't still.

His Circle was broken.

His rhythms, perturbed.

And it was his own doing.

His ego, long buried, had shot up like a rocket.

And its fires singed him still.

Wantonly, he had let this be.

Of course, he coulda stopped himself.

He still could.

But his mind, wretched instrument, was made up.

'Cause he let it.

He wished to let it burn.

He knew the consequences.

Out of orbit. Like a shooting star.

He was sad.

For the first time.

He looked up at the heavens bristling over with fire and water.

Emptiness sucking in emptiness.

It is how stars die, he thought.

CHAPTER FIFTY-NINE

What a day.

He was out of his cosmic dream.

Like being naked, suddenly, for the first time.

Out of his cocoon.

He shivered.

Now he had rejoined the world.

His dad would have been happy.

Not his mom.

Maybe even Shiela…

But no use thinking of her.

She was part of some plan he didn't know of.

So do people become pointers, instruments, and catalysts.

They pushed you to fulfill your Destiny.

He didn't like it.

He wished he didn't have a destiny.

But he knew he had.

He had woken up.

The trance was broken.

He let the tears fall.

Idle tears.

Born of Fear.

The One Thing he had never known.

CHAPTER SIXTY

When he was eleven, there had been a fire at their home.

He was upstairs.

His mom was out on the porch, lighting a barbecue.

His dad wasn't home yet.

Within minutes, the house was ablaze.

Screaming sirens, the fire engines rolled up.

Everyone was shouting.

My baby, cried his mother, he's trapped upstairs.

The firemen spoke to him through bullhorns.

Come out to the window, Junior. There are firemen waiting with a net.

He sat looking down at the fire.

It was awesome.

Like the end of the world.

He was mesmerized.

Jump, jump, they cried.

He looked down at them from his perch.

They looked small.

But mighty riled up.

His mama was in hysterics.

Jump, Junior, she shrieked.

Jump, kid! shouted the fire-chief.

He smiled at his mother.

It's okay, Mama. I'm fine.

His mama fainted.

The firemen hollered.

He looked back at the fire, and the collapsing house-frame.

Then he looked down at the crowd. He could see some of his schoolmates there.

Jump, Junior, shouted Eric.

Medics were helping his mama. She needed him.

He stepped into the air, and fell into the net.

They rushed him to the hospital for burns.

He hadn't felt them.

Nor had he felt any fear.

CHAPTER SIXTY-ONE

When he was fifteen, his schoolmates took him out for a spin.

It's Saturday night, they said, we go blow up town.

3 boys in a big car, drinking beer, past midnight.

Here, try it, said the boy who was driving.

No, he had said. It smells icky.

Hear that, Eric, it smells icky…!

The boys guffawed.

Okay, Junior, we're gonna get you something nice to drink. You like a soda?

Uh-huh.

Good: come on guys, let's go get Junior somethin' to drink.

The car veered in front of a convenience store.

The boys jumped out.

Come on, Junior.

They all went in.

Eric went up to the night clerk.

Got any garbage bags?

Uh…

Ain't on the shelf.

Maybe there's some in the back. I'll go see.

The clerk walked back to the store room.

Come on, said Eric.

The boys grabbed six-packs of beer.

And a grape soda for you, said Eric, tossing a large, plastic bottle in his hand.

Let's go!

Hey wait…!

The clerk was back.

Stop!

The car took off. He was still standing there, holding the bottle.

The clerk jumped on him, knocking him down.

You wait right here, scumboy, said the clerk, sticking his gun in his cheek. One move – and you're history.

He took out a mobile phone and dialed.

The Cops came.

So, kid. Where's your friends?

He just stared at them.

I don't know.

Didn't wait for you, huh? Too bad…come on, let's go.

They took him to the station, and called his parents.

It was bad.

His dad was furious. Not because he had done something bad.

But 'cause he had gotten caught.

But he had felt no fear.

CHAPTER SIXTY-TWO

Now he knew what it was.

There was nothing he could do.

Just Shiela.

Could she have changed everything?

No. Perhaps he was just asking to be born again.

Normal-like.

Like ordinary people.

See, he had lived another life.

It was peaceful.

Not happy.

Nor sad.

Just so.

Now, he could feel everything.

No wonder the world appeared crazy.

It was driving him nuts, too.

What to do? It was a question which had never occurred to him.

Now it had.

And the small of his stomach hurt to ponder it.

To be, was so easy.

To do, was difficult.

To choose, simply nightmarish.

CHAPTER SIXTY-THREE

But he had.

And the day's journey had to be completed.

His fate had caught up with him.

Shiela was only an instrument.

The rain stopped, as if on cue.

He closed his eyes.

He could see the mountain, the valley, and the silver stream.

And the sky that watched over them all.

Could anything be more beautiful?

The sun broke through again.

He opened his eyes.

Time to move on.

He took one last look at the pond.

It looked like a silver bowl of jello.

He looked at the park.

It looked stark and desolate.

Time to forget.

He walked on.

CHAPTER SIXTY-FOUR

He thought of his cat.

He hoped the coffee hadn't hurt her.

Shakespeare was a special cat.

She never miaowed.

Never ate nothing, but one brand of cat chow.

Shiela had named her Shakespeare.

He had just wanted to call her kitty.

Shakespeare sat by the window and looked out.

Much like he did.

He wondered what she thought, about everything.

He talked to her, too.

And she would just stare intently into his eyes.

She's in love with you, said Shiela.

And I with her, said Junior.

You're serious, said Shiela.

Yes, he said.

Shakespeare didn't like Shiela.

She never even looked in her direction.

She only likes her master, said Shiela drily.

I am not her master, he said.

CHAPTER SIXTY-FIVE

The apartment owner didn't like pets.

I hate pets, he said.

Why? he had asked.

Nasty critters, messin' up everythin', and tearin' the place down, poopin' all over the goddam place…

My Shakespeare never does none of those things.

Shakespeare…is that the name of that mangy little critter?

She ain't mangy…she's an awful pretty cat.

Animals belong in a zoo, not in people's homes.

Oh, no, Mr. Babbitt, they don't. Ain't nice to cage 'em up.

Your cat is caged in here, ain't she?

Well, yeah…wasn't my idea…Shiela brought her in.

Shiela…holy cow! How many critters live in this place, dang it!

Just me and Shiela and Shakespeare, sir.

Is that right? I'll tell you what…I have a good mind to toss you all out of this building, but here's the next best thing: you're gonna pay a hundred dollars more per month in rent for taking in boarders…pay up, or get out.

Okay.

Okay?

Yes, Mr. Babbitt, that's fine.

Well…okay…but if I see, or hear, or smell that cat of yours anyplace in this building other than your apartment, you'se all out, d'you hear?

Yeah, Mr. Babbitt, sure thing.

Okay, I need that hundred – make that a hundred-fifty, in advance. Now.

CHAPTER SIXTY-SIX

Funny thing about animals.

They really weren't what people took 'em to be.

They had a world of their own.

A silent world, for the most part.

That's what he liked about 'em.

You could be awful quiet with them, and they didn't mind.

They sort of shared the space.

People weren't like that.

People…oh, well…

But animals needed space too.

And it was wrong to take that away.

They just sat, or fretted, and waited to die.

Like people in cages.

No, it was very wrong.

Space.

It was a condition.

For all.

He knew what had to be done.

CHAPTER SIXTY-SEVEN

Lenny was on the phone.

Shiela came in the door.

Lenny watched her, still talking.

Shiela looked up at him.

Lenny put the phone down.

What?

He's not home.

So?

Shiela looked at him.

Shouldn't have fired him.

Aw, he had it comin'…sooner or later.

Didn't need it now.

Say, what's this…you still feeling sorry for him?

Maybe.

Well, don't. He don't think like us.

That's for sure.

What's that supposed to mean?

I wanna see the boss.

What for?

Just do.

Shiela!

Shiela walked up to the door marked 'Boss'.

Lenny watched.

The door closed behind her.

Say, Shiela…well, well, well…

Why'd you fire him?

Fire whom?

Come on…

Junior…that kook? Well…'cause he's good for nothin'…

That's bull…you paid the poor slob less than a minimum wage, Sam…

Hey, Shiela, take it easy…you know he don't care how much we pay him…

You guys rake in plenty…d'you have to go stiff a sap like Junior? So I start wond'ring: n' yeah, you been stiffin' me, too…I ain't gettin' no five percent like you promised…I cook your books for you…that's worth a lot of dough…

Sure it is…I promise…

You're a goddam liar! I'm cuttin' out of this crap…

What?

Yeah: I don't wanna be your stooge no more. This joint sucks.

Hey…!

And so do you, Lenny, and all you losers…one day the cops is gonna blow all o' you away…don't say I didn't warn ya…

Shiela!

G'bye.

CHAPTER SIXTY-EIGHT

Shiela stormed out.

Lenny ran after her.

Wait…what the heck is wrong with you?

With me…? You wouldn't know, Lenny…you wouldn't get it if I rammed it down your throat…

What the heck you so mad about?

You wanna know…do you?

Yeah. I do.

Okay. I'll tell you. When I dumped Junior and moved in with you, I thought maybe, you 'n' me had something special going…y'know…romantic like…with just the two of us…

Of course we do, babe…

Bullshit! Bullshit! I said just the two of us, Lenny.

What's that supposed to mean?

I mean I ain't sleeping with Sam just so you can make it with the boss, you sunuvabitch…

Hey, wait a minute…as I remember it, you'd just as soon mess around with Sam as with me…

That ain't true…

Oh, yeah?

Yeah. I was ready to fix your books, n' more. But it was for you, Lenny. You read me? Now…it's over. I wised up: you're a jerk.

I'm a jerk! Hey, you ain't no Mother Teresa yourself…

Maybe not…but I ain't no fool…sooner or later, you'd be setting me up to take a fall. I'm leavin'. God, I was a fool.

Shiela, wait.

If I were you, I'd quit, Lenny. You're over your head in this. It'll be twenty-five years in Sing-Sing if…

Sam came out as she slammed the door behind her.

You gotta win her back, Lenny.

I know…

Do it now…we can't take any chances… one mistake and…

Okay…just give me some time…

We may not have any if…

Okay, okay…I'll take care of it…trust me…

You better: you cut her into this…

Take it easy, Sam. It's gonna be alright.

CHAPTER SIXTY-NINE

Impulses.

He had them at times.

He knew what they were.

But he always swept them aside.

Now, he was letting them come in.

And they were taking over.

That was what was frightening.

There were voices, too.

But he had never listened.

Until now.

And he was afraid.

They were talking.

And urging.

And he was growing weaker.

No.

He should not.

He must not.

But…

There was nothing left.

No one.

Except Shakespeare.

CHAPTER SEVENTY

You didn't pay your taxes, said the IRS man.

No, sir.

Why not?

I didn't work that year.

Oh…then how'd'you live?

I had a few hundred dollars left over.

You lived a year on a few hundred bucks!

Yes, sir.

How about rent?

It was my mother's house.

Transport?

Didn't go no place.

Food?

Just bread n' milk n' stuff…

Junior…

Yes, sir.

I think you're shittin' me…

No, sir.

I think you are…you on drugs, Junior?

No.

You a pusher?

No.

Maybe both…it don't look good…your neighbors tell me you're a loner, and a strange feller generally…

I…

Tax evasion's a crime, Junior…we got a warrant to search your house for any undeclared assets…

They searched his house and found a small cache of marijuana.

The judge fined him a thousand dollars, plus a citation. Shiela paid up.

It's okay, she told him, it was mine.

CHAPTER SEVENTY-ONE

One day, they came and took his mother's house away from him.

Seemed his dad had some debts.

Good they took it after his mother had died.

She had taken in laundry to pay for the house after his dad got killed.

She'd have been awful sore.

Shiela was upset, too.

Now we'll have to rent a place, she said, crossly.

He didn't care.

His mama went. So could the house.

It was all the same.

He wouldn't have known if Shiela hadn't told him about the savings his mother had left.

I've been taking care of it for you, she told him. I'll make it grow.

Okay, he said.

He was fortunate.

Shiela knew all about smart investments.

CHAPTER SEVENTY-TWO

Only now he discovered he had no money.

Not even to feed Shakespeare.

That was not right.

What was he to do?

It didn't matter for his sake.

But Shakespeare!

He'd have to ask someone.

Maybe Lenny.

Or Sam.

Or Shiela?

Time to go.

But he still had a few things to do.

Yes.

That was imperative.

It had to be done.

He had waited too long.

CHAPTER SEVENTY-THREE

Shiela's going away was bad.

But not as bad as when he came home one day to find her in bed with Sam.

Go away, Junior, Sam had said.

I won't.

Come on, Junior, do as he says, said Shiela.

She had no clothes on.

Beat it, said Sam. Go on, shoo.

He kept staring at her.

She looked beautiful.

You look beautiful, he said.

Shiela covered herself.

Go away, Junior, she said, softly.

I love you…

Okay, now leave.

But I live here.

It's okay. Come back later.

Okay, but you sure look beautiful.

He left.

CHAPTER SEVENTY-FOUR

Okay, he was no fool.

So they made a monkey out of him.

So what?

Didn't bother him.

They weren't really bad people.

People were never really bad.

Just angry, or sad, or afraid, or hurt.

Which made them do bad things.

He knew that.

He couldn't change any of that.

It was just the way it was.

So why bother?

You just waited for them to get over their bad selves.

And be normal again.

'Course, some took longer than others.

And others never did.

It was okay.

It was just the way it was.

No point fretting over that.

He could wait.

Forever.

'Least, that's what he had always thought.

But today he was feeling impatient.

Like he couldn't wait that long.

Like it was time.

CHAPTER SEVENTY-FIVE

Dr. Manx wanted to give him pills.

No, sir, he had said.

But they could make you well.

I am well, Dr. Manx.

Junior.

Yes, sir?

I want you to take these pills. Every day. Without fail. And if you don't, I'll have to send you away from home to be in a nursing home, where they'll make sure you take 'em.

Away from mama?

You bet.

I don't wanna be away from her.

Well, then…

Okay…I'll take them.

There's a good boy. Here, take the first dose now.

He took the pills home, and then threw them away.

Every week, Dr. Manx examined him, and his teacher talked to him.

They said he was getting better.

After 12 weeks, they pronounced him well.

You see, Junior, modern medicine is miraculous. It has cures for everything.

Am I cured, sir?

You bet. And now you can go and live a normal life.

Okay. Can I ask you somethin'?

By all means. Go ahead.

What's the matter with me?

Ah, my boy; now that's a deep question: the matter with Junior. Someday you'll be old enough to understand.

Yes, sir. Can I go now, sir?

Yes, of course. Goodbye, Junior. Be good, now.

Later on, he told his mother about the pills.

She looked cross at first, but then hugged him.

You did well, my son, she said.

CHAPTER SEVENTY-SIX

Mama always stood by him.

So, it was upsetting when she had a fight with his dad.

His dad often came home drunk.

When drunk, he slapped his mama around.

He didn't like that.

Once, he threw himself between his mama and his dad, and his dad had swept him off the floor with one swipe.

At that, his mama went crazy.

She ran to the drawers, and came out with his dad's rifle.

Swear to god, I'm gonna kill you today.

His dad looked scared.

Hey…Mary…be careful…it's loaded…

You sunuvabitch…you touch my Junior, and I'll…

And she shot off the gun.

His dad jumped up and ran out the house, as she shot off again and again.

He cried out: Don't, mama: you'll hurt dad.

And she stopped, but with the gun still pointed at his dad.

His dad kept running. And didn't return home for weeks.

He never hurt mama or Junior again.

He don't really mean it, she told him later. But drinks gets on his nerves.

CHAPTER SEVENTY-SEVEN

They got on his nerves, too.

One drink, hours ago, and he still felt dizzy.

Or maybe it was something else.

He couldn't place it.

You'll know it when your heart breaks, said his mama.

Did your heart break, mama?

His mama stopped with the laundry.

Did it, mama?

His mama didn't say nothing.

She looked away.

Soon, she wiped the corners of her eyes with her sleeve.

Be quiet, Junior, she said.

He was quiet.

Mama was sad.

Why?

Heartbreak.

Was that what was bothering him?

He thought of the day he saw Shiela in bed with Sam.

Was that heartbreak?

He thought of mama.

Of course he knew who broke her heart.

It was his dad.

Who drank, came home, and beat up on her.

And rarely brought home any money.

He had always known.

It's life, his mama might have said, had he asked her.

CHAPTER SEVENTY-EIGHT

It's small things that matter, not the big things. Take care you don't forget, mama had said.

Small things. What were they?

Jobs?

Love affairs?

Homes?

She hadn't told him.

He didn't know what the big things were, either.

You'll figure it out, she had said.

So he'd have to.

No money in his pocket.

Was that a small or a big thing?

How about Shiela and Lenny?

Some things you let go, she had said.

Which ones?

It could be pretty confusing, getting them all right. And what if you made a mistake?

One mistake, and you're dead out there, his dad had said.

That couldn't be true…could it?

Well, his dad had died in a train collision.

Someone had made that one mistake.

It could be true.

Small things.

Shakespeare was a small thing.

He'd have to worry about her, no matter what.

That cat chow.

Couldn't forget that.

CHAPTER SEVENTY-NINE

Junior, Shiela called him softly.

She was very drunk.

Yeah?

Gotta tell you something…something important…

He just looked.

I'm not…what you think I am.

I don't understand.

You think I'm your friend?

Yes.

No, Junior. It's wrong. It's all wrong.

What's wrong?

Everything!

Shiela tossed the empty vodka bottle against the wall, where it shattered into a hundred bits.

He wondered whether Mr. Babbitt would show.

Don't you understand?

No.

Go away, Junior. Go far away from me. I'm no good for you. Find yourself someone good for you.

You're very good!

God, you're stupid! Junior, listen to me: I'm a taker, not a giver. Don't you see that! Are you blind?

No.

You gotta be. I'm...I don't know how or when it happened...but I turned into a...a bad girl...a very bad girl...I wasn't always this way, Junior, you gotta believe me...

I do!

I crossed the line, Junior...and I wish I didn't...it's not what I wanted to be...

Shiela sobbed, and he didn't know what to do.

Know what I wanted to be?

No.

I wanted to be an Avon lady...you know what an Avon lady is?

No.

She's someone who makes people happy. She goes door to door with a magic kit-bag of beautiful things. Powders and perfumes and pretty little things like that. And she takes time with people. Listens to them. Feels their needs, and gives them what they need. It's beautiful, Junior. Then I wanted to marry and have a family and...

Shiela sobbed again.

But they wouldn't give it to me...said I was an alcoholic. It was bad for their image. You think I'm an alcoholic, Junior?

No.

'Cause you're stupid. That's exactly what I am. And you know why?

No.

'Cause I feel good. It's the only way I feel good, Junior, can you understand that?

Yes.

No, you can't... you can't understand anything. You had a home and a mother that took care of you all your life...you had it easy, Junior...and all I had...shoot, what am I saying... Jesus Christ! I gotta go...

Shiela got to her feet and went to the door...

Bye, Junior...see you later...don't wait up for me.

CHAPTER EIGHTY

So Shiela was sad, too.

Why was everyone sad?

His dad, his mom, Shiela…

All except he.

How could they not know?

Anytime he wanted, he could be away in his valley.

With the sun, the sky, and the silver stream.

He could never be sad.

He could always go away.

Why couldn't they?

Why couldn't Shiela?

Was he really different?

No.

It couldn't be.

Of course he knew.

They let their Circles strangle them, instead of letting them just spin.

And the circles would close in, and suck up all space.

Leaving them suffocating.

That was sad.

Perhaps he could tell them.

So they would understand.

Would they?

He wondered.

CHAPTER EIGHTY-ONE

Curious how animals in zoos ignore each other.

Like they know these are not their real environs.

Predator, prey – it didn't matter.

They all had one Great Preoccupation.

And he knew what it was.

He wondered why people didn't notice such things, when they went to zoos.

The children laughed and played in their innocence.

Even the adults relaxed, sort of…

But the animals never really joined in.

The elephant swayed from side to side, dreaming.

The tiger looked glassy-eyed over the top of the ogling crowd.

The panther paced endlessly.

What a pathetic menagerie.

Perhaps their restlessness was a metaphor or something.

For people, too.

CHAPTER EIGHTY-TWO

It was getting closer.

He could feel it.

That great Big Circle that surrounded him for years had gently lifted off, and gone skywards.

He watched it float away, without emotion.

It was like letting go of a life-buoy.

Now he was without his own special rhythms.

The aura that warmed him had been let go.

Voluntarily.

Now he was like anyone else.

Without moorings.

Anchor.

Or rudder.

He felt a little unsteady.

Like vertigo.

Perhaps he would fall.

He must try not to.

It was very important.

CHAPTER EIGHTY-THREE

The little zoo that graced the park stood to one side.

The animals, long forgotten by people who stopped visiting, were dying slowly and silently.

The polar bear, ten years in a concrete stockade, barely moved.

He paused by each and talked to them.

They did not respond.

He sat and watched them all, silently.

The rain fell again.

It was almost dark, though only mid-day.

In the distance, the traffic sounds turned into a static blur of noise.

He felt lulled.

Perhaps not they but he who was in a cage, only bigger.

And who, or what, would free him then?

At mid-day, the keeper would come in a van, and throw food at them.

The animals would barely stir, not seeing the keeper or the food.

Of course, the food would get eaten sometime. It had to be.

He rose.

This was the day.

Things had to be done.

CHAPTER EIGHTY-FOUR

Sam walked over to Lenny.

So?

No dice.

This ain't good.

I know.

Gotta do something.

What?

Well, go find her.

Where…this is a big city.

Must be someplace, someone she knows.

I don't know…

You don't know…goddammit, you brought her to this, and you don't know…

Wait…wait, I've got it.

What?

She's out looking for Junior.

So?

Well, there ain't too many places he can go.

Okay: so get out there, and look.

Okay.

And Lenny.

Yeah.

This is serious.

I know.

Don't mess up.

There was a knock at the door.

It was Junior.

CHAPTER EIGHTY-FIVE

Shiela let herself into Junior's apartment.

Well, it was hers too.

Until recently.

She popped some pills.

Then she looked for her bottle.

And found it.

A few minutes later, she started to feel better.

And think clearly.

There was only one way to cut all this crap.

It was to tell Junior all.

But where the heck was Junior?

Well, she would find out.

It wouldn't take long.

Junior was easy.

Too easy.

It was the matter with Junior.

Shakespeare rubbed up against Shiela's legs.

You're as dumb as he is, said Shiela, patting her head.

CHAPTER EIGHTY-SIX

It must be the park.

Shiela walked to the pond, where the ducks were swimming.

It felt cold.

She sat down by the tree.

So, this was where it all began.

So very long ago.

There he had been, sitting in a trance.

There she came running.

Wham!!

What a chump!

To roll over, like a log, and fall right into the pond.

Even the ducks must have laughed their tail-feathers off.

Shiela smiled, and shivered.

It was cold.

The vodka wasn't warming her at all.

It started to rain.

Shoot, she said. I hate to get wet.

Cold and wet, it really was too much.

Where the heck was Junior?

She shoulda brought the bottle with her.

But there wasn't much left.

Well, she would have to sit right there, and wait for him to show.

She wasn't going to go staggering around, looking for him in the rain.

She didn't much feel like movin'.

She wished she had her jacket.

She closed her eyes.

A little shut-eye could do her a lot of good.

CHAPTER EIGHTY-SEVEN

Shiela had a little dream.

It was about herself as a little girl.

She was raised in an orphanage.

She remembered waking in the middle of the night in a cold sweat, most every night.

Fear.

It was dreadful.

Years before she got over those.

The drinking helped.

She had been abandoned as a baby.

The police found her, none too soon.

She could have died of exposure.

The doctors saved her life.

Which the matrons then ruined for her, at the orphanage.

She was just naughty at first.

But then turned mean.

And cold.

And hard.

She had sex when she was eleven, with the mailman.

He was still in jail.

She was the seductress.

She had sex with other girls.

Even when they didn't wish it.

Okay, so she was bad.

She was a loser.

And she knew it.

So what?

The dream was very real.

She woke up, shivering, in the dream.

It was cold.

And raining.

And she had chugged a liter of straight vodka.

CHAPTER EIGHTY-EIGHT

Shiela had meant to rob Junior blind.

And she almost had.

But then a funny thing happened.

She started to care.

And feel.

Not too much, she wasn't stupid.

But just enough to stop short.

It was too easy.

Like a godsend.

And god had some making up to do, as she recalled.

Junior's mother's bank funds were far from a king's ransom.

But they were enough.

And she had swiped it all.

She wouldn't starve to death no more.

Bingo!

But then life got a little complex.

She wanted more than food and drink.

Like someone who could make her feel good.

She thought may be Sam could.

Or Lenny.

But it was not to be.

They just made her wanna drink more, afterwards.

Strange, but not Junior; the goop, the sucker, the fall guy.

He seemed appealing.

She wanted him.

She needed him.

It was too weird.

Not sex, or anything.

But holding him close was warmer than Sam and Lenny together.

It was awful cold.

Boy, did she miss her Junior.

CHAPTER EIGHTY-NINE

So she found out that Sam and Lenny moved narcotics, behind a business front.

Poor Junior was the innocent drop man who made their deliveries.

Couldn't be a better gopher.

They were happy when they found out she could keep books, besides sleeping with them.

She learnt both at the orphanage.

She was just as good at either.

But it was no small scam they were running.

They were shooting high.

And she knew it could get rough.

She knew why they fired Junior.

They couldn't depend on him, should he stumble onto the game.

At any rate, she had her nest egg.

No sense risking all for a bit more.

So it had to be chucked.

Simple.

She woulda left town.

Except for Junior.

Dammit, he was getting in her way again.

Maybe it was destiny or something.

CHAPTER NINETY

She laughed, in her dream.

Maybe they were losers, all.

The whole goddam rat-pack.

Even Junior.

No, she could not bring herself to believe that.

Junior was different.

Junior was good.

Junior was clean.

God, it made her feel lousy.

Like it was all her fault.

But it wasn't.

She had it pretty rough.

A little girl in a big town.

Trying to survive.

Couldn't get rougher.

Sure she got pushed over, real bad, a few times.

But it didn't matter.

She learnt.

From every knockdown.

And here she was, still on her feet.

Well, sort of.

And that was saying something.

Wasn't it?

She could take anything, except feeling cold.

And guilty.

And alone.

And now she was feeling all three.

Where the heck was he?

She had to get it off her chest.

Dammit, Junior, where are you?

CHAPTER NINETY-ONE

What have we here? said Lenny.

Yeah, what? said Sam.

Junior didn't say nothin'.

Just stared at them.

He looked kinda wild. His clothes were torn. His face and arm were bloody and scratched up.

Where the blazes have you been?

Is Shiela here?

No…

Okay…

Wait.

Junior turned around.

I said wait.

Lenny strode up.

We need to find Shiela. You gotta help us.

Junior walked on, and Lenny grabbed him.

Let me go, said Junior.

Hold on a second, said Lenny, tightening his grip, did you hear what I just said?

Junior shook him off. Lenny, losing balance, fell sideways on to a steel desk top, hitting his head on its edge.

Junior, unlike Sam, didn't see him bleed.

Jesus Christ!

Sam came running over and grabbed Junior.

You dumb sunuvabitch!

Sam swung a heavy metal disk at Junior, catching him in the face.

Junior felt and tasted his blood.

Sam piled on to Junior; as Junior stuck out the file he was carrying, folded in a newspaper, protectively.

It rammed Sam plumb in the stomach.

Sam slumped to the floor.

Junior looked at the file which had cut through all the cage locks at the zoo, and tossed it.

He looked over at the two men. They were motionless.

He couldn't figure it.

But he couldn't dally, either.

He had to find Shiela.

And tell her.

He ran out.

CHAPTER NINETY-TWO

The rain started again.

He was bleeding from his face. And arms.

But he kept running.

Passersby made way for him, staring.

He ran to the park.

Police cars, flashing lights, and blaring sirens were congregated some distance away by the little zoo, with people milling around.

There was a lot of shouting and hailing.

Junior stopped, and looked instead toward the pond.

And the tree.

She was there!

Junior ran up.

Shiela, he cried.

Shiela was asleep under the tree.

Sweet Shiela!

He knelt by her, and ever so gently caressed her head, so she wouldn't awaken.

She rolled over sideways, limp.

Junior stood up.

She was not asleep.

Shiela was gone.

She too was free.

CHAPTER NINETY-THREE

He sat by her, cradling her head in his lap.

He talked to her.

Did I ever tell you about my valley? he asked.

It has a silver stream.

A mountain.

And a clear blue sky…